CUENTO
DE LUZ

To Manuel and Rosario, my parents, for everything.
To Nati, my sister, for everything.
— F.N.

To my family, my home.
— Z.C.

Water and tear resistant
Produced without water, without trees and without bleach
Saves 50% of energy compared to normal paper

The Map of Good Memories
Text © 2016 Fran Nuño
Illustrations © 2016 Zuzanna Celej
This edition © 2016 Cuento de Luz SL
Calle Claveles, 10 | Urb. Monteclaro | Pozuelo de Alarcón | 28223 | Madrid | Spain
www.cuentodeluz.com
2nd printing
Title in Spanish: El mapa de los buenos momentos
English translation by Jon Brokenbrow
ISBN: 978-84-16147-82-3
Printed in PRC by Shanghai Chenxi Printing Co., Ltd. February 2017, print number 1604-8

THE MAP OF GOOD MEMORIES

Fran Nuño ✤ Zuzanna Celej

Zoe had lived in the city since she was born. But now, because of the war, she had to flee with her family and take refuge in another country.

The night before she left, she decided to do a little experiment.
She spread out a map of the city on the table,

ZOE'S HOUSE

GRANDMA'S HOUSE

THE SQUARE

THE ICE CREAM PARLOR

THE SCHOOL

THE PARK BENCHES

THE PARK

THE BOOKSHOP

THE BASKETBALL COURT

THE LIBRARY

THE SWINGS

and started to mark all of the places where she had spent her happiest times in the ten years of her life.

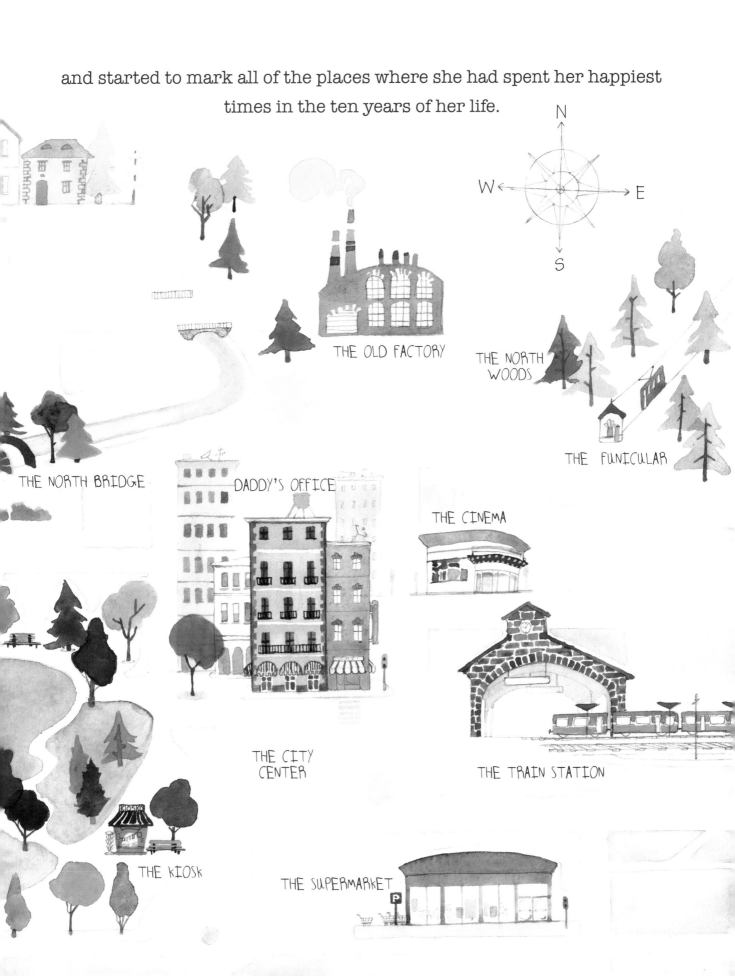

THE OLD FACTORY

THE NORTH WOODS

THE FUNICULAR

THE NORTH BRIDGE

DADDY'S OFFICE

THE CINEMA

THE CITY CENTER

THE TRAIN STATION

THE KIOSK

THE SUPERMARKET

First, she marked the house where she lived.
Here she had learned to walk and spoken
her first words. Her room had always
been a wonderful place, full of games and
daydreams. Her home had become a place
full of good memories.

Then she marked the place where she was
at that particular moment—her school.
While she did it, she ran through the names
of her teachers and her favorite classmates.

She'd been at school for so long! But Zoe was
never bored, and she loved learning new
things every day.

Then she marked the library and the bookshop,
which were still in her neighborhood.
They were two places she absolutely loved.
The people who worked there introduced her
to books that filled her with all different
kinds of emotions.

Their shelves were full of real treasures.

The park in the middle of
the city was another place of good memories.

Its trees and bushes made her feel like she
was in another world. It was an island of
green filled with different
kinds of animals.

She'd spent many Sunday mornings there,
playing on the swings, listening to people
playing music, and riding her bike.

Zoe loved going to the movies, so she
drew a circle around her favorite cinema,
and remembered all the films she'd
enjoyed there.

She also thought about the candy
counter, the big seats, the lady who
showed you to your seat with a flashlight
. . . and the magic of the big screen!

The river was also marked on her map.

Her favorite place was next to the
North Bridge, where sometimes she
could see fish in the water,
and a family of ducks who loved
eating crumbs of bread.

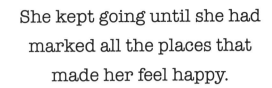

She kept going until she had
marked all the places that
made her feel happy.

After looking at the points scattered
over the map, she started to
connect them with a red pencil,
in the order she had discovered them
throughout her life.

She wanted to know what kind
of shape would appear by joining all
the good memories together.

When she looked up, Zoe could
not believe what she saw!

ZOE'S HOUSE

GRANDMA'S HOU

THE SQUARE

THE ICE
CREAM PARLOR

THE PARK

THE SCHOOL

THE PARK BENCHES

THE BOOKSHOP

THE BASKETBALL COURT

THE LIBRARY

THE SWINGS

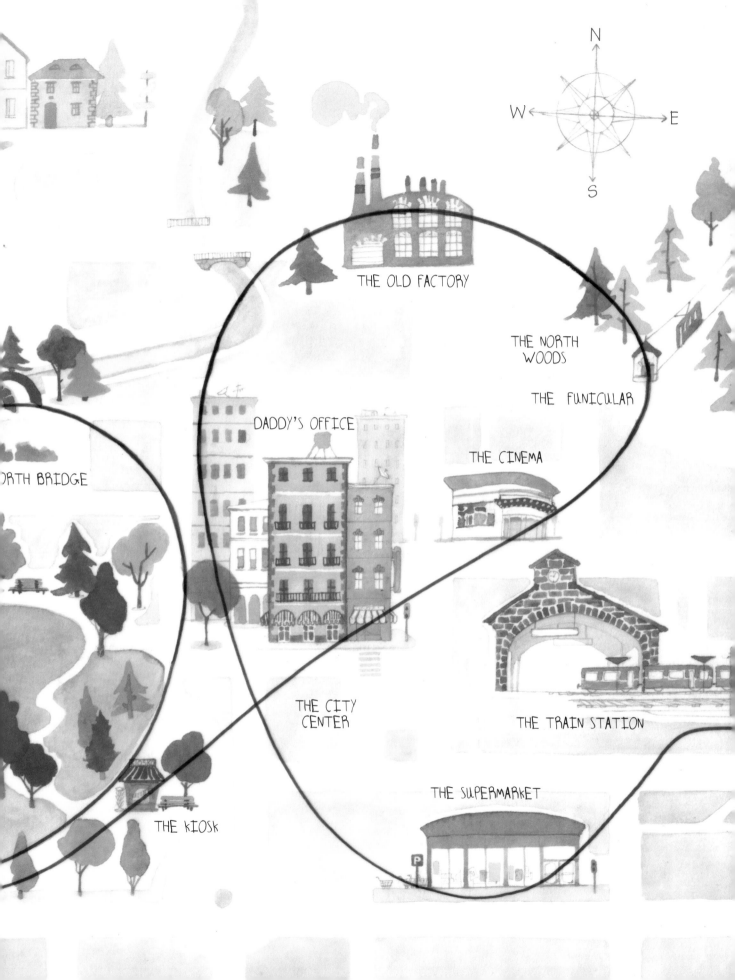

The shape on the map made
the letters of her name!

Zoe didn't know if this had happened
by accident, or if it meant something.
Perhaps it was the city's way
of saying goodbye to her.

What she did know is that wherever she went,
all of the wonderful memories
she had would always be with her.

Zoe tucked the map of good memories
neatly into her suitcase.

It was the map of a city she was sure
she'd return to one day.

Author's note

"...to see the modern world with the eyes of the child I once was, with the eyes of the children I meet."
—Philippe Delerm

More than anything else, this book is about saying farewell. Zoe, the main character, says goodbye to the city where she has always lived. Because of the war, she has to flee with her family to another country, and has no idea what will become of her. Her name, which is Greek in origin, means "life," and through her memories we discover some of those good times, those simple pleasures that life sometimes gives us, and where true happiness may be found. The happiness that Zoe, unfortunately, is about to lose.

I have always enjoyed books that talk about these simple, daily pleasures, which encourage the reader to think about their own and make a list. I cannot deny that I would love the readers of this story to do the same experiment that Zoe does with the map of her city, and then discover the result.

I would like to end with the hope-filled words that Anne Frank once wrote in her diary: "One day, this terrible war will be over..."

—Fran Nuño